Reading together is fun with
SHARE-A-STORY

A series specially designed to help you encourage your child to read. The right and left-hand pages are arranged so that you take turns and the story develops as a conversation. Fresh, humorous stories illustrated by top artists ensure enjoyment for everyone!

'Revolutionary . . . done with as much good psychology as good humour ... Pat Thomson has contrived a set of readers likely to brighten bedtime for all parties' — *Mail on Sunday*

MY FRIEND
MR MORRIS

by
Pat Thomson
Illustrated by
Satoshi Kitamura

PUFFIN BOOKS

Hello, Mr Morris,
Mum baked you a cake.
She is bringing it round for you
in a minute.
What are you doing?

I'm just looking through
these catalogues.
I thought I might like to send
for a cat.

Mr Morris!
I know what a catalogue is.
It's a list of things to buy.
It has nothing to do with cats.

Oh, I see.
I'll just have to settle
for a trunk, then.
My elephant could do with a new one.

Mr Morris!
You can't get an elephant's trunk
from a catalogue.
Those things are big cases.
You pack your clothes in them.

Yes, I know.
My elephant is going on holiday.
What about a pair of bedsocks, then?
I'm sure my bed gets cold in the night.
It has four legs
so I'll need two pairs, won't I?

Of course not, Mr Morris.
Beds don't need socks.
They are for *your* feet.
You had better stick
to hot water bottles.

I don't want anything sticky
in bed, thank you.
There's a good clean walking-stick.
That would be useful.
I could send it out for a walk
while I have a nice lie-down.

It won't go on its own, Mr Morris.
I think you are being
a little bit lazy.

All right, I'll speed things up.
Here some running-shorts.
I could watch them
racing round the garden from my chair.
My goodness, I feel quite tired.

I can see I had better
find you something easy.
What's this thing for dusting?
A feather duster?

Now, that's a good idea.
I haven't dusted my feathers for ages.
I could dust the parrot.

Mr Morris!
You couldn't.
It might start giggling
and fall off its perch.

All right. I couldn't stand
a giggling parrot, anyway.
Let's choose a pair of headlights.
I haven't got two heads,
but one light would be useful.

Headlights are for cars, Mr Morris.
That's why you need two.
You would look like a lighthouse
with your shining head.

I like to be useful.
Just for fun, though,
let's order some pet food.
I've never thought
of making a pet of any food before.
I'm sure my dog wouldn't mind sharing
his basket with a nice cake.

And I know why, Mr Morris.
You wouldn't keep *that* pet for long.

Very true.
I'll get something more solid.
This wooden chest might be useful.
I could beat my chest like a gorilla
and it wouldn't hurt a bit.

I'd like to see that, Mr Morris.
Can you do it now?
Be a gorilla and beat your chest.
You could stand on your chair
to do it.

Well, perhaps not.
Let's have something more restful.
I'd prefer a hat-band.
It would have to be a big hat, but then,
I do love music.

You can't have that sort of band
on your hat, Mr Morris.
It would be nice if you could.
We could have a party
here in the garden.

Why not?
We could have a party, anyway.
We can afford it
because I haven't bought anything
from this catalogue.

I like your idea of a catalogue, Mr Morris.
I wish there really was somewhere
which sold all those funny things.
I like your muddles.

We could make our own catalogue.
Get your muddles from Mr Morris!
Come on, you're pretty good
with the coloured pencils.

Yes, just think, there would be cats,
trunks, bedsocks, walking-sticks,
shorts, feather dusters, headlights, pet food,
all sorts of chests,
       and the loudest hat-bands in town.

Here comes your mum with my cake.
We'd better put the kettle on.
Now, I wonder.
Could she bake us a few sponges
for the bath?

PUFFIN BOOKS

Published by the Penguin Group
Penguin Books Ltd, 27 Wrights Lane, London W8 5TZ, England
Penguin Putnam Inc., 375 Hudson Street, New York, New York 10014, USA
Penguin Books Australia Ltd, Ringwood, Victoria, Australia
Penguin Books Canada Ltd, 10 Alcorn Avenue, Toronto, Ontario, Canada M4V 3B2
Penguin Books (NZ) Ltd, Private Bag 102902, NSMC, Auckland, New Zealand

On the World Wide Web at: www.penguin.com

Penguin Books Ltd, Registered Offices: Harmondsworth, Middlesex, England

First published by Victor Gollancz Ltd 1987
Published in Puffin Books 1999
1 3 5 7 9 10 8 6 4 2

Text copyright © Pat Thomson, 1987
Illustrations copyright © Satoshi Kitamura, 1987
All rights reserved

Printed in Hong Kong by Wing King Tong

British Library Cataloguing in Publication Data
A CIP catalogue record for this book is available from the British Library

ISBN 0–140–38887–7

Other Share-A-Story titles

BEST PEST
Pat Thomson and Peter Firmin

CAN YOU HEAR ME, GRANDAD?
Pat Thomson and Jez Alborough

DIAL D FOR DISASTER
Pat Thomson and Paul Demeyer

NO TROUBLE AT ALL
Pat Thomson and Jocelyn Wild

THANK YOU FOR THE TADPOLE
Pat Thomson and Mary Rayner

THE TREASURE SOCK
Pat Thomson and Tony Ross